To...........................

Happy Halloween!

Love.............................

Prepare If You Dare

A Halloween Scare in GEORGIA

Written by Eric James

Illustrated by Marina Le Ray

HOMETOWN WORLD

Prepare, if you dare,
for a **Georgia-wide** scare,
A night of pure terror to whiten your hair,

A tale full of sights that are best left unseen.
You ready? You sure?
This was my Halloween.

The werewolves
howled loudly.
The moon shone so bright.
I stayed in my bedroom,
the curtains shut tight.

My heart started pounding,
my knees felt so weak,
But, being a brave kid,
I just **had** to peek.

I pulled back the curtains. My mouth opened wide.
An army of monsters had gathered outside!
They staggered and stumbled and lurched down the streets
With bags full of cookies and candy corn treats.

Emerging from sewers and houses and stores
Came creatures and critters with ravenous roars.
Then more came along from all over the state.
They filled up the streets at a dizzying rate!

From Athens, Savannah, Atlanta, and Rome,
They gathered together outside of my home,

To go trick-or-treating
for one **spooky** night,
And seek out the living,
then give them a **fright**.

The thunder clapped loudly with terrible booms.
The witches dodged lightning and clung to their brooms.
The two-headed doggies tried chasing their tails,
And banshees let loose with their hideous wails.

The vampires hung out
on the street in their gangs,
And grinned, just to show off
their pearly white fangs.

JUST
MARRIED IN
GEORGIA

The mummies moaned loudly and swayed side to side,
While Frankenstein stomped about town with his bride.

An alien race from a faraway sun
Came looking for Roswell, but chose the wrong one.

They soon fell in love with our warm Southern charm,
Completely forgetting they came to do harm.

The swamp monster came out of OKefenoKee.
He **roared** and he **roared**
till his voice went all croaky.

He felt so embarrassed, he hid out of sight.
(A squeaky swamp monster just doesn't sound right!)

The creepies were crawly, the crazies were crazed,
The zombies from Johns Creek had eyes that were glazed.
The ogres from Macon were ugly as sin,
With big bulging noses and warts on their chin.

The ghouls danced around but were lacking in soul,
The gargoyles could rock, and the headless could roll!
Although the whole spectacle seemed to spell doom,
I foolishly thought I'd be safe in my room!

But then something happened
that made my heart jump.
From somewhere below me
I heard a big THUMP!

I froze for a moment, as quiet as a mouse.
Yes, I could hear noises from INSIDE THE HOUSE!

I put on my slippers

and pulled on my robe.

I shook like a leaf

but I don't think it showed.

Then, slowly but surely,

I crept down the stairs,

Preparing myself for the
biggest of scares.

My hands trembled wildly.
I opened the door.
I still shudder now
at the horrors I saw.
The stereo spat out
some hideous sounds
As dozens of monsters
jumped madly around.

The sight was horrific. It made my skin crawl.
These monsters were having their
Halloween Ball!

And right in the middle, one monster loomed tall,
The **hairiest, scariest monster** of all...

He turned round and saw me.
I fell to my knees.
"I'm not very tasty,
so don't eat me, please!"

He beamed ear-to-ear
and broke free from the huddle,

Ran over,
and gave me a...

BIG

MONSTER

CUDDLE!

"At last!
We have found you!" he said with a smile.
"From Dalton to Douglas,
we've looked for a while.

BEST COSTUME IN

GEORGIA

I ♥ GEORG

"We came here to give you your wonderful prize."
He held up a trophy in front of my eyes.

"A prize? And for me?"

I replied with a grin.
"But what did I enter and how did I win?"
"You've won the first prize for the costume you're wearing!
It even scares me, and I'm tip-top at scaring!"

"This isn't a costume. I'm just dressed as me!"

"Exactly, the scariest thing you can be!

A small human child, with a cute button nose.

Your teeth are so shiny, you've only ten toes.

No hair on your face and no horns on your head.

The whites of your eyes are not glowing or red!

A bone-chilling costume! A horrible sight!

A worthy ensemble
for Halloween night!"

We partied together
until the moon set,
A Halloween night
that I'll never forget.

And next year I won't
want to hide in my bed.
The monsters won't scare me,

I'll scare

THEM

INSTEAD!

Written by Eric James
Illustrated by Marina Le Ray, Amerigo Pinelli,
and Natalie & Tamsin Hinrichsen
Designed by Sarah Allen

Published by Hometown World,
an imprint of Sourcebooks Kids
P.O. Box 4410, Naperville, Illinois 60567-4410
(630) 961-3900
hometownworld.com
sourcebookskids.com

Date of Production: February 2022
Run Number: 5025154
Printed and bound in China (OGP)
10 9 8 7 6 5 4 3 2